IMAGINE THAT™

Licensed exclusively to Imagine That Publishing Ltd
Tide Mill Way, Woodbridge, Suffolk, IP12 1AP, UK
www.imaginethat.com
Copyright © 2019 Imagine That Group Ltd
All rights reserved
0 2 4 6 8 9 7 5 3 1
Manufactured in China

Written by Lloyd James
Illustrated by Barbara Bakos

ISBN 978-1-78700-111-4

A catalogue record for this book is available from the British Library

For Alix, for being the braver of the two,
and for our son Charlie, the mightiest splash of all! x

THE MIGHTY SPLASH!

An under-the-sea superhero story

Written by Lloyd James

Illustrated by Barbara Bakos

Once upon a time, in the deep, blue ocean, there lived an octopus called Gus.

All Gus wanted was to be as brave as his favourite superhero, **'The Mighty Splash'.**

But there was one little problem ...
He was scared of ...

EVERYTHING!

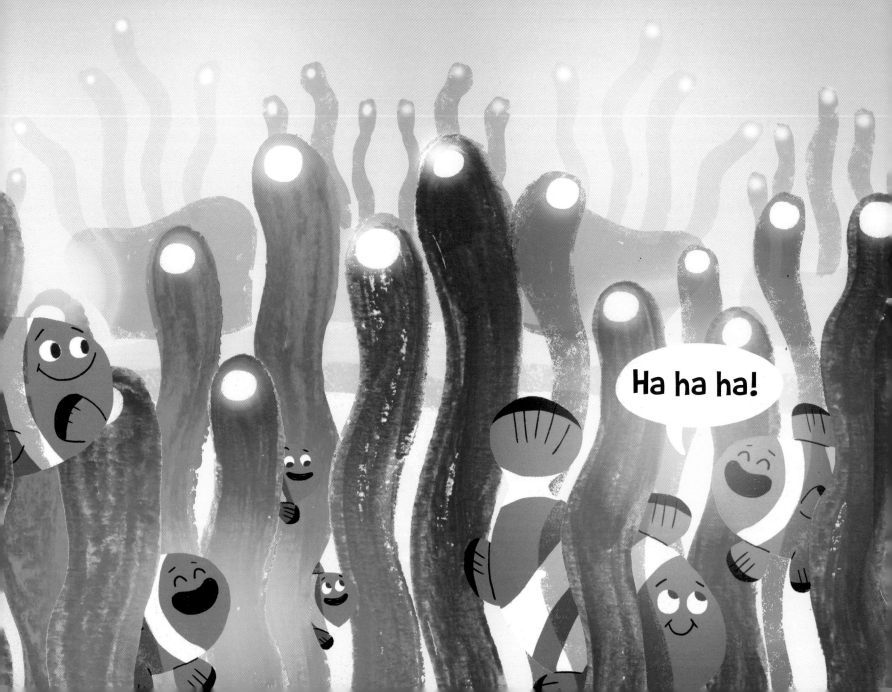

If there was a storm, Gus hid.

If there was a shadow,
Gus swam away.

And at night, when it was dark, Gus trembled and cuddled up to his teddy!

At school, Gus dressed up as a superhero and pretended he was as brave as The Mighty Splash, but all his friends laughed at him and called him names.

'Being brave is hard,'
Gus thought to himself sadly,
as he changed colour and hid
behind a rock.

Then, one morning, Gus had an idea. He would go on an adventure to find The Mighty Splash and ask him how to be brave!

After packing his favourite seaweed sandwiches,
Gus left the safety of his home and set off on his way.

Gus swam over colourful reefs and through dark, scary caves.

He swam past spooky sunken ships
and beneath big **CRASHING** waves!

He swam and he swam and he swam until his little tentacles could swim no further.

But there was still no sign of The Mighty Splash!

By now, Gus was a long, long way from home
and he was starting to feel a bit scared.
'Maybe it wasn't such a good idea
swimming off on my own,' he thought.

Then, as he rested by a rock, Gus heard a frightened cry,
and saw a flash of white teeth and a huge grey fin.
A group of seal pups were trapped by an enormous shark!

'So, what are you going to do?' asked a voice. Gus looked down in surprise and saw a tiny old crab.

'Me?' quivered Gus. 'What can I do? I'm just a little scared octopus.'

'Everyone gets scared from time to time,' said the crab. 'Even sharks! Did you know that some sharks are scared of the dark?'

'Scared of the dark ...' thought Gus. 'That's it!'

Quick as a flash, Gus zoomed between the shark and the seal pups, and soon, a big black cloud surrounded them all. Gus had used his special octopus ink to turn the water as dark as night!

The shark was surprised. In fact, the shark was so scared that it turned and swam away as fast as it could.

Once the ink had drifted away, the seal pups
thanked Gus and swam off to find their mums.

'You were right,' said Gus to his new friend. 'That shark really was scared of the dark!'

'Come on, let's get you home,' chuckled the crab.

Gus and the crab travelled back beneath big crashing waves ...

past spooky sunken ships ...

through dark, scary caves and over
colourful reefs until finally ...

... Gus was home!

Before he knew it, Gus was being squeezed tightly in his mum's arms. All eight of them!

'Thanks for returning Gus home safely,' said Gus' mum to the old crab. 'You must have been very scared, Gus.'

'Everyone gets scared from time to time,'
said Gus. 'Even sharks!'

'Don't be silly,' said Gus' mum.

And when Gus turned round to thank his new friend, the tiny old crab was gone in a ...

Mighty Splash!